JAMES MAKES A CHOICE

BY **THALIA WIGGINS**
ILLUSTRATED BY **DON TATE**

magic wagon

visit us at www.abdopublishing.com

Published by Magic Wagon, a division of the ABDO Group, PO Box 398166, Minneapolis, Minnesota 55439. Copyright © 2012 by Abdo Consulting Group, Inc. International copyrights reserved in all countries.

Calico Chapter Books™ is a trademark and logo of Magic Wagon.

Printed in the United States of America, North Mankato, Minnesota.
102011
012012

Text by Thalia Wiggins
Illustrations by Don Tate
Edited by Stephanie Hedlund and Rochelle Baltzer
Cover and interior design by Neil Klinepier

Library of Congress Cataloging-in-Publication Data
Wiggins, Thalia, 1983-
   James makes a choice / by Thalia Wiggins ; illustrated by Don Tate.
      p. cm. -- (Making choices. The McNair cousins)
   Summary: When money becomes tight in the McNair household, James forms a local gang of kids who steal the things they want from the local stores, while his cousin Greg is working hard for the money to buy things.
   ISBN 978-1-61641-634-8
   1. Cousins--Juvenile fiction. 2. Decision making in adolescence--Juvenile fiction. 3. Gangs--Juvenile fiction. 4. Theft--Juvenile fiction. 5. Trinidad--Juvenile fiction. [1. Cousins--Fiction. 2. Decision making--Fiction. 3. Gangs--Fiction. 4. Stealing--Fiction. 5. Trinidad--Fiction.] I. Tate, Don, ill. II. Title.
   PZ7.W63856Jam 2012
   813.6--dc23
                                                2011027716

Contents

James's Bad News

James turned over in his bed and yawned. A summer breeze blew from his open window, bringing in the scent of early morning flowers. He felt that it was going to be a great day in the Trinidad community of Washington DC.

James imagined the fun he would have playing basketball with his friends. All of a sudden, Grandpa Joe called from below. It sounded important.

James sucked the air between his teeth and rolled out of bed. What did Grandpa want now? Minutes later, his brother, Charles, joined him in the hallway. Together, they made their way to the living room.

"I hope this won't take long," James muttered, dropping onto the sofa next to his cousins, April and Greg. He folded his arms and glared at his grandfather.

"Times are getting hard around here," Grandpa began. "Your grandmother has to get a job to help out with the bills."

April's eyes widened. She glanced at their grandmother, who nodded in agreement.

"That means that from now on, we'll have to count on you four to help out around the house. You'll no longer be getting your allowance unless you do your chores. Your grandmother and I have to work hard for our money. We feel that you all should do the same."

"That's not fair!" James exclaimed. His fist pounded the armrest. He could not believe what he heard. "You expect us to do chores? Why can't Grandma just clean after she gets home from work?"

"How dare you!" April shouted.

Grandpa raised a hand in warning to April. He eyed James.

"Your grandmother and I are not as young as you are," Grandpa said. "Since you were young, you've eaten the food we buy you. You've worn the clothes we buy you. Now you are old enough to help out and keep the house clean."

He turned and smiled at Grandma Rose. She handed him the list of chores, keeping a copy for herself. Grandpa handed them to Charles, who passed them down. When James read his list, his eyes narrowed.

"Wash the dishes. Set the table. Cook dinner. Take out the trash . . ." He flung down the paper and folded his arms again. "I'm not doing it. You can't make me!"

"You're right." Grandpa smiled coolly. "I can't make you, but I won't pay you, either."

"Fine." James got up and stomped out of the room and up the stairs. Seconds later, he slammed his bedroom door.

James swore loudly in his room. Even though he was twelve, he'd never done chores before. His grandparents had just given him money whenever he needed it. Now they expected him to clean and dust? What a waste of time! He would rather hang out with his friends.

An hour later, James stormed out of the house. He walked up the street until he came to the recreation center. Moochie, his best friend, sat on the steps with a group of boys James's age.

"What's up, Moochie?" James said.

"Hey, James!" The boys bumped fists.

"Man, my grandpa says we have to do chores for an allowance now! Can you believe that?" James shook his head.

"You call that chump change he gives you an allowance? My brother can pay you twice that much in a day for less work!" Moochie chuckled.

James's eyes widened. If he could make twice as much by doing less work, he was all ears.

"What does he do?" James asked.

Moochie looked around as if he didn't want to be overheard. He moved closer to James and lowered his voice.

"Let's just say he pays boys to . . ." Moochie whispered, "uh . . . move merchandise for him."

James's stomach dropped at Moochie's words, but he thought of the money he could make. "Well, what are we waiting for? Let's meet him!"

James and Moochie walked down to the corner store. A group of young men stood in front. James knew some of them. They were always in trouble with the police.

"Yo, Ken!" Moochie called. A young man twice as old as James walked over to them.

"Hey, Mooch." He punched his little brother's arm playfully.

"This is James." Moochie pointed to James. Ken nodded at James and looked him over.

Moochie lowered his voice and said, "He's looking for work."

Ken looked around to make sure no one heard them.

"Cool," he said. He looked James in the eye. "Be at our house at eight o'clock sharp."

"Alright." James nodded, trying to look cool, but his stomach was in knots.

Later that night, James snuck out of his bedroom window and headed for Ken's house.

"Right on time." Moochie smiled at James as he opened the front door.

Ken sat on a leather couch in the living room. He was playing video games on a new video game system with a big-screen TV. The living room was packed with boxes. James's eyes roamed the boxes of stereo equipment, video game systems, electronics, and TVs. He guessed what Ken's line of business was—stealing items and reselling them.

James felt uneasy. He swallowed hard, knowing what his grandpa would think.

"We're businessmen," Ken explained. "We have to find a way to survive. If no one is going to help us, we must help ourselves." He put an arm around James like an older brother. "Are you in?"

James wanted to say no, but he was too scared. *I just want to make money. I just want to make money,* he told himself.

"When do I start?" he asked coolly.

Ken grinned. "Now. Here's what I want you to do."

James Goes Bad

What am I doing? James asked himself as he peeked behind the shelf in the electronics store. Moochie stood by the counter, distracting Joe, the store owner.

James tucked the package under his shirt. Immediately he began to sweat. The plastic stuck to his skin. He held his breath and made his way to the front door. He tried his best to walk normal.

"Did you find what you were looking for?" Joe asked.

James stopped and stared into Joe's eyes. He quickly thought of a lie.

James swallowed. "Naww . . . I was looking for batteries."

Joe sighed and looked at the clock on his wall. "Sorry, son. Truck's late. Come back in a couple of hours." James nodded and left.

As soon as he rounded the corner, James let out a deep sigh. He lifted his shirt and peeled the sweaty box from his body. He looked it over.

"What would Grandpa say?" he wondered aloud.

He looked down at the MP3 player he had just stolen. He might have taken money from Greg or an extra cookie without asking, but he'd never stolen anything from a store.

"You did it!" James jumped at Moochie's shout. Moochie slapped James on the back.

"Piece of cake," James smirked. His throat felt dry.

Moochie laughed. "I'd hate to see the look on Joe's face when he discovers that's missing."

James looked at the price. It would've taken him a month to save for it with his allowance.

On the way back to Moochie's house, James decided he would tell Ken that he'd had second thoughts. He didn't want to steal. Stealing was wrong.

I'll tell him as soon as I see him, James thought.

James's thoughts went out the window when he saw the wad of money Ken pulled out of his pocket. He handed James his pay. It was more than a month of allowances!

"Thanks, man!" James tried not to sound too eager.

"No problem. Be here tomorrow. I got another job for you," Ken said.

A few weeks later, James could hardly move around in his room because there was so much stuff. He couldn't decide if he wanted to play video games on the big-screen TV or watch music videos on the smaller one. He decided to listen to one of the new rap CDs he'd stolen the day before.

Suddenly, he heard a loud voice over his headphones.

"James!" Greg called.

Frightened, James quickly turned. It was just Greg. Why hadn't he locked his door?

"What!" James yelled, lifting one of the headphones off his ear.

Greg continued. "We're having pizza tonight. Grandpa wants to know what toppings you'd like." He turned and looked around.

"Where did you get all of this stuff?"

"Oh, you know, from my boys," James said, ignoring the fear in his stomach. "They asked me to hold these for them." He waved his hand around the room. "I have to make sure they work."

"Where did *they* get the stuff from?" Greg asked.

"What are you, the police?" James jumped off the bed. He pushed Greg out of the room.

"Don't ever come back in here!" he snarled. "And tell Grandpa I want pepperoni!" He slammed the door in Greg's face.

James leaned against the door, breathing hard. He wondered all night if Greg would tell Grandpa about his room.

The next day, James met Moochie in front of the video game store. Moochie started to tell him about the new game that came out when they were interrupted.

"Yo! James!"

James turned to see Troy, one of the neighborhood boys walking toward him and Moochie.

"What?" James turned to Troy.

"I hear your cousin Greg is trying to be a Boy Scout," Troy teased. "He's going around the neighborhood cutting people's grass and helping old ladies across the street."

All of the boys nearby snickered.

"Why don't you shut up?" James got into Troy's face. Troy flinched but held his ground.

"What are you gonna do if I don't shut up?" Troy hissed.

James did not answer. Instead, his fist connected with Troy's chin. Down he went.

"Wow!" Moochie exclaimed. The group of boys moved closer to see more of the fight, but Troy jumped up and ran.

"Next time you better watch your mouth!" James called. The boys laughed.

"Man, you hit him so hard, I felt it!" Moochie rubbed his jaw. The boys agreed.

"We should call you Rock because you hit hard like one!" Moochie added. There was another cheer of agreement.

James smirked. "I like it!"

Moochie looked over his shoulder. "Hey, Rock. There's Greg now. He's going into the video game store." He pointed behind them, and James turned in time to see his cousin walk into the store. James frowned.

"He's probably checking out that new game," he guessed.

Moochie chuckled. "Bet you he buys it before you can get it!"

James shoved Moochie playfully. "Please. All I need is five minutes in

that store, especially if Mike is working there alone."

Minutes later, Greg left the store and spotted his cousin. He walked over to them.

"Hey, James," Greg smiled excitedly, "did you see the new basketball game?"

"Yeah, I saw," James said, leaning against someone's car. He looked at his boys and smiled. They laughed.

"What's so funny?" Greg asked. He stopped smiling.

"I was just telling my boys that I'm gonna get that game way before you do. In fact, I am going to *beat* that game way before you even save enough to buy it!"

Greg folded his arms. "How are you going to get the game if you don't have a job?"

"Don't worry about it." James pushed him hard. Greg stumbled, but he kept his balance. He started to walk away.

"See you at home, Greg the Goofy!" James shouted. Moochie and the boys laughed.

James remained silent. He had just thought of something. *If my cousin is known as Greg the Good, does that make me James the Bad?*

Bad Versus Good

That afternoon, James and his boys stole the new basketball video game from the store. James couldn't wait to rub it in Greg's face.

When he got home, James burst in the front door as Greg came downstairs. James smirked.

"Guess what."

"What?" Greg asked as he tried to walk by him.

"This!" James shoved the game under his nose.

Greg's eyes widened. He tried to reach for the game, but James pulled it out of his grasp.

"Sorry," James sneered. "I have to test this out, see that it works." He tried not to laugh at Greg's expression as he went upstairs.

"Wait!" Greg called after him. "Can I at least play it after you're done?"

James turned and waved the package. "Hey, I'm a businessman. This is merchandise. You can have it . . . for a fee."

"But I'm your cousin!" Greg shouted.

James shrugged and moved up a step. "Grandpa said that times are hard. Since I'm not getting allowance . . ."

Greg made a face and turned away. James chuckled to himself. *How's that*

for being good? he thought. *All of that hard work and for what? I'm making more money in two days than he makes in two months!*

James closed his door and sat down. Then he had an idea. *What if Greg joined the gang? Greg knows just about everybody and they trust him. Greg could distract them*

while we fill our pockets. We could make some real money!

James continued to think of his idea as he went downstairs. He noticed that Greg was still on the couch.

"Greg the Goofy—" he started to say.

"Don't call me that!" Greg snapped.

"Whatever." James waved his hand dismissively. "When you want to make some real money, let me know."

"What?" Greg sat up. "You mean join your gang of hoodlums?"

"They're not hoodlums," James said harshly. "They are businessmen. And I better not hear you call them that again."

"You guys go around causing trouble and stealing from hardworking people. Just because they call you the Rock doesn't mean they are your friends. How are you businessmen?" Greg asked.

"We just have a different way of making money than you do," James said. He put his hands in his pockets and leaned against a wall. "It's better than all that work you do. You could make three times what you make mowing lawns if you hang out with us."

"No," Greg said firmly. "I'll never join your gang of thieves. I like helping people. It makes me feel good. You'll never understand."

"Have it your way, Greg." James headed for the front door. He shook his head.

Maybe I can convince him another way, he thought as he walked. Then he smiled. He had another idea.

A Bad Idea

"Yes! Yes!" James shouted as he jumped to his feet. He laughed as the video game tallied his score. He had just beaten the game!

Time to make an announcement! he told himself. He threw open Greg's door.

"Yo, Greg!" he yelled.

Greg groaned from under the covers, "What is it?"

"I beat the game!" James hollered.

"So?" Greg asked shifting the covers.

"Oh, please," James said. "You know you want the game. Come on, I'll let you have it cheap."

"No!" Greg sat up in bed. He glared at James. "You stole that game. You can tell me whatever you want about it being business, but I'll never buy anything you stole!"

"Fine," James chuckled. "Just remember that while you're picking up dog poop, I'm making some real cash!"

With that, he slammed Greg's door. He cursed as he went downstairs. He didn't want to put his plan into action, but Greg left him no choice.

James left the house and walked to meet up with Moochie and the boys at the recreation center.

"Man, what's up with Greg?" Moochie asked after James told him about Greg.

James shrugged and gritted his teeth. "He says he actually likes doing good. It's as if doing good is better than making money."

Moochie, Nick, and Jeff's eyes widened. Then they shook their heads.

"He probably needs a little persuasion," Nick said, holding up a clenched fist for clarity.

"Nah." James smiled an evil grin. "I have another plan that will give Greg a taste of what the bad boy life can be."

A while later, they were standing in front of Joe's Electronic Store. James looked inside the display window and spotted Greg.

"Yep," James said, pointing inside. "I thought I heard Greg tell Grandpa he'd be here today." They all turned and noticed Greg looking at them. James waved, but Greg rolled his eyes and went back to dusting the shelves.

"Poor Greg the Goofy," James said.

The boys quietly went inside the store. Joe was talking to Greg a few aisles down. James's friends quickly helped themselves to Joe's merchandise. When James heard Joe and Greg coming, he gave them the signal.

Joe noticed them and scowled. "Get out!" he snarled. "I don't want any trouble!"

"I'm just here for Greg," James said, trying to look innocent.

"Yeah, right," Greg said, unconvinced. "You can wait outside then!"

James wanted to strangle Greg for talking to him like that. But he thought of his plan and held back.

He smiled. "Come on, boys." He led the way outside.

Greg came out later with a nervous look on his face. He looked back to Joe watching him and the boys. Greg waved to him and started walking. James chuckled and shook his head.

"Man, why are you all hunched over?" he demanded. "I'm not going to jump you for a few dollars! Anyway," James stopped walking to face Greg, "I just want to thank you."

"What did I do?" Greg looked scared.

"You kept old Joe busy while we helped ourselves to a few of his goods."

"What?" Greg gasped. He eyed James's friends' shirts and suddenly realized what happened.

"No!" Greg groaned. "How could you?" He looked like he wanted to attack James.

James handed a box to Greg. "This is for being a great lookout."

"I wasn't your lookout! You used me!" Greg shouted.

"Quiet!" James hissed, shoving the package into his hand. "Making cash would be much easier if you worked with us. You know all the people around here and they trust you. You could—"

"Never!" Greg hollered.

"Okay," James said soothingly. "But this is for you anyway." He motioned for his boys to follow him. They hurried across the street, leaving Greg alone.

"What did you give him?" Moochie asked.

"The video game he wanted. That should tempt him." The boys agreed.

James's Dream

James did his best to slip in the window quietly. He did not want to wake Grandpa. James shut his window and peeked behind the curtain. He scanned the street below to make sure no one was watching.

He had to do that now because the whole neighborhood knew what he and his boys were up to. Hardly anyone trusted them. Whenever they walked in stores, people watched them. It made stealing more difficult, but James still had not been caught.

Then James thought of all the trouble he got into. *I'm just trying to make money,* he thought. *Times are hard. I have to help myself. No one is going to do it for me.*

The last time James saw Grandpa, he'd had to run. Grandpa was ready to punish him. Grandpa hardly believed James now and never trusted him. This hurt James's feelings.

He always asks me a dozen questions, James thought as he eased himself under his covers. *It's not like I'm asking him for money now. I'm making my own. Besides, if he knew half of the stuff I did, he would kill me!*

James hoped he wouldn't have another nightmare about him being in jail. Lately, he had those dreams but decided to ignore them.

I'm having too much fun, James thought. *I'm unstoppable! It's Greg who needs to wise up and join us. We could be making so much money. He needs to come to his senses.* James drifted off to sleep.

James dreamed that he was back in second grade. The kids teased him because he didn't live with his parents. They beat him up because he wore old, tattered clothing. His grandparents could not afford to buy him the latest styles. James had to fight to earn respect.

Then he dreamed of Moochie, Nick, and Jeff. They looked up to him and made him the leader of the gang. He loved every minute of it. He felt like he belonged somewhere versus the outsider that he felt like at home. He felt like he had . . . a family.

James's dream shifted to one of the talks that his Grandpa gave him after someone told him James was stealing. He checked James's room, but James had already moved everything out.

"I want to believe that what I hear on the street isn't true," he told James, "that you're not out there stealing."

"I'm not," James lied. "I'm just helping out Moochie's brother moving, uh, boxes around."

"You mean that young man I see on the street corner causing trouble? You're helping him?" Grandpa's voice rose.

"Grandpa, how do you know if he's causing trouble? He's just a businessman. What you're hearing are rumors."

Grandpa shook his head. "James," he began, "whenever you do bad things, bad things happen to you as a result. You may think that you're having fun, making money, but sooner or later you will get caught and get in trouble."

Grandpa eyed James sternly. "And you better not let me catch you doing anything." James shrugged.

"Why can't you be more like Greg?" his grandmother asked. "He works hard helping people."

James scowled. "Why do I want to be a Goody Two-shoes like him?"

Besides, he thought, *I can make more money and earn more respect doing my own thing than Greg ever will!*

James smiled to himself in his sleep. He loved the respect his friends, Ken, and the older boys gave him. He felt at home on the streets.

Bad Boy Busted!

"Yo, Greg!" James came into the living room the next afternoon. Greg looked up.

"Want to come with me and my boys to the video game store? That idiot Mike will be the only one there working today. Maybe you could . . ."

Greg cut him off. "I returned the game."

"What?" James felt the heat rise on the back of his neck.

"I returned the game." Greg stood up and faced James. "And I'll never, ever join your gang. So, stop bugging me!"

James raised his fists, ready to beat Greg senseless, but April and Grandpa came into the room.

"What's going on?" Grandpa shouted.

"Nothing, Grandpa," James said quickly. "I'll see you later, Greg the Goofy," he hissed under his breath. Then he marched out the front door.

Within minutes, James had told Moochie and the boys what Greg had done.

"What?" Moochie's eyes widened. "He actually returned the game?"

"Yeah." James shook his head. "I can't believe it!"

"He didn't say where he got it from, did he?" Nick asked.

"I don't think so." James frowned. "But he'll answer to me if he did!"

The boys headed to the video game store. It was the weekend, so Mike already had his hands full with customers.

Mike noticed them come in and shook his head. He turned back to a customer he was helping.

The boys went through their usual routine. Moochie made sure that Mike was distracted.

James quickly stuffed a game under his shirt and signaled to the boys. Casually, they made their way to the door, making sure that Mike was focused on a mother and her son.

James was almost out the door when he heard a voice that made his skin crawl.

"Hold it right there, young men!"

They all turned to see a security guard emerge from the back room.

He spoke into a walkie-talkie in his hand, keeping an eye on the boys. He said, "That's right. Four of them. At the video game store."

James's heart pounded.

Mike chuckled and spoke aloud, "Finally caught you boys red-handed."

"We didn't do anything!" James exclaimed.

"Oh yeah?" The security guard walked to them. He pointed to all the video cameras in the store that the boys had ignored.

"Empty your pockets," the officer commanded.

Suddenly, Jeff pushed past James and ran out the door. He didn't get far. James turned around and saw four officers heading toward the store. One of them had Jeff by the arm and led him inside.

"He made us do it!" Jeff cried as he came in. He pointed to James. "He's the ringleader!"

James looked incredulous. "Oh yeah?" He tried to approach Jeff to pound him, but an officer grabbed him.

"Empty your pockets," the officer said again.

James braced himself and pulled the game from under his shirt.

It's over, he thought, *I finally got caught.* Tears of disappointment fell down his cheeks.

The officers put the boys in handcuffs. James started to sob. The handcuffs seemed to make the situation real—he was in big trouble.

Consequences

A week later, James could not believe he was still alive. Even though he was home, he could not get the image of the juvenile detention center out of his mind.

His dreams were haunted by visions of bars on the windows, hard benches, and Moochie sobbing in a corner.

The worse of it all was Grandpa. He remained cold and distant toward James. Whenever they were in a room together, Grandpa did his best to ignore James.

James could see the hurt and disappointment in Grandpa's eyes. As much as James tried to act like it didn't bother him, secretly he had to admit his own heart was broken.

How can I hurt the man who has taken such good care of me? James thought as Grandpa drove him to court. *He does so much to make sure I have food and clothing, but all I do is cause trouble.*

Stepping into the courtroom was like stepping into a nightmare. James did not know what to expect. He sat next to Grandpa and looked around the room.

There were many boys James's age in the room waiting for the judge to decide their fate. *Will this be my life?* James wondered. *Will I always be coming here to stand before a judge? Is this what I want?*

James heard his name called. Grandpa nudged him in the ribs. He stood up to go before the judge.

"James Steven McNair?" The judge looked him in the eyes.

"Yes, sir?" James thought his heart would burst in his chest.

"You are charged with shoplifting. You will be sentenced to fifty hours of community service."

"Yes, s-sir," James stammered.

Two weeks later, James moaned, "Man, I wish I hadn't started stealing!" He had just come from his community service assignment. He flexed his fingers, which hurt from picking up litter on the side of the road.

"I have to pick up trash after school and on the weekends! I have no time to hang out with my boys!" James complained.

Even worse, James had to deal with some of the other boys. Many of them had to do community service for crimes far worse than shoplifting. The boys were meaner, angrier, and larger than James. They picked on James when the guards weren't looking. He fought almost every day.

"Serves you right," Grandpa said behind a newspaper. "That's what happens when you commit a crime."

James fell silent. He hunched his shoulders and stared at his food. Grandpa took pity on him. He looked at the scratches on his grandson and knew that he had to say something. He put his hand on James's shoulder.

"I know that you have had it hard, James," Grandpa began. "But you are making it even harder when you do bad things, like stealing. You end up hurting people who could help you in the future."

James tried not to let the tears form in his eyes. He stared really hard at his mashed potatoes. He felt that Greg had been right all along by helping the neighbors and doing chores for them. He was the one with the real respect.

Greg would be able to hold his head up high, while James would have the shame of being the bad boy. James wondered if he could ever be like his cousin.

"I just want you to think about the life that you are living," Grandpa said. "I also want you to know that I love you."

"I love you, too," added Grandma.

"Yeah, even if you are a rebel," April agreed, rolling her eyes.

James nodded, blinking back his tears. He couldn't remember the last time Grandpa had told him that he loved him, but it felt good. He felt like a member of his own family. He felt that he actually belonged.

After dinner, James went to his room. Instead of going straight to sleep, he crawled in bed and stared at the ceiling.

All he could think about was the fact that he must choose between his family on the streets and his real family at home. He tried to find reasons to be like Greg and to stop doing bad things.

It made him cringe to think about all the people he'd stolen from and how he would have to earn their trust again. He imagined the look of approval on Grandpa's face, and how good that would make him feel.

Next, he thought about Moochie and his other friends. James loved being a leader and feeling accepted by the boys of the neighborhood, even if they did commit crimes.

Ken looks out for me, he thought. *Moochie is like a brother to me. We have fun together. My friends on the streets accept me for who I am and not who they want me to be, unlike my grandparents.*

James still hadn't decided what to do by the time he fell asleep.

The End

Making Choices
Greg the Good

Every decision a person makes has a consequence. Greg made some decisions that earned him the nickname Greg the Good. Let's take a look:

Decision: Greg chose to help his neighbors to earn extra money.

Consequence: Greg earned the respect of his family and the people in the neighborhood.

Decision: Greg chose to return the stolen video game and stay out of James's gang.

Consequence: Greg was not in the group of boys arrested for stealing!

Making Choices
James the Rock

Every decision has a consequence. James made some decisions that got him in trouble. Let's take a look:

Decision: James chose to help his friends steal items and sell them to get money.

Consequence: James was watched closely by his family and the people in the neighborhood.

Decision: James and his group continued to steal.

Consequence: The group of boys were arrested!

About the Author

Thalia Wiggins is a first-time author of children's books. She lives in Washington DC and enjoys imagining all of the choices Greg and James can make.

About the Illustrator

Don Tate is an award-winning illustrator and author of more than 40 books for children, including *Black All Around!*; *She Loved Baseball: The Effa Manley Story*; *It Jes' Happened: When Bill Traylor Started to Draw*; and *Duke Ellington's Nutcracker Suite*. Don lives in the Live Music Capitol of the World, Austin, Texas, with his wife and son.